See Mouse Run

KT-430-533

For Mum and Dad
SG.

See Mouse Run

Sally Grindley and Priscilla Lamont

Piccolo Books

The farmyard was quiet,
Not a creature stirred,
Not a sound could be heard,
Then suddenly . . .

See Mouse run
with a squeak, squeak, squeak.

Mouse is frightened.
TAP, TAP. What's that noise?

See Duck run
with a quack, quack, quack.

Duck is frightened too.
RAT-A-TAT. What's that noise?

See Cat run
with a miaow, miaow, miaow.

Cat is frightened too.
BING, BONG. What's that noise?

See dog run with a woof, woof, woof.

Dog is frightened too.
THUD, THUD. What's that noise?

See Pig run
with an oink, oink, oink.

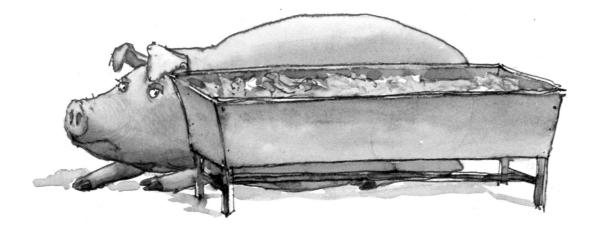

Pig is frightened too. THUMP, THUMP, THUMP.
What's that noise?

See Goat run with a baa, baa, baa.

Goat is frightened too.
BOOM, BOOM, BOOM. What's that noise?

See Cow run
with a moo, moo, moo.

Cow is frightened too.
BANG, BANG, BANG. What's that noise?

See Horse run with a neigh, neigh, neigh.

Horse is frightened too. BANG, CRASH, BOOM, BANG, BOOM.
What's that noise?

Horse is frightened
Cow is frightened
Goat is frightened
Pig is frightened
Dog is frightened
Cat is frightened
Duck is frightened
Mouse is frightened

What's frightening them?
It's getting louder.

Is it Farmer Tasker on his big red tractor which rumbles and clatters and grinds and clunks?

No, he's a long way away working in the fields.

Is it Billy Tasker on his brand new motor bike which splutters
and grumbles and hisses and roars?

No, he's gone to market to buy some more sheep.

It's little Tommy Tasker going DRUM, DRUM, DRUM.
And following behind him is his hot cross Mum.

She's yelling and she's shouting that he's making too much noise.
But Tommy cannot hear because . . .

. . . he's making too much noise!

First published 1985 by Hamish Hamilton Children's Books
This Piccolo edition published 1987 by Pan Books Ltd,
Cavaye Place, London SW10 9PG
10 9 8 7 6 5 4 3
ISBN 0 330 29362 1
Text copyright © 1985 by Sally Grindley
Illustrations copyright © 1985 by Priscilla Lamont
All Rights Reserved
Printed and bound in Great Britain by
Springbourne Press Ltd., Basildon.
This book is sold subject to the condition that it
shall not, by way of trade or otherwise, be lent, re-sold,
hired out, or otherwise circulated without the publisher's prior
consent in any form of binding or cover other than that in which
it is published and without a similar condition including this
condition being imposed on the subsequent purchaser